Copyright © 2019 by Cale Atkinson

All rights reserved. Published in the United States by Doubleday,
an imprint of Random House Children's Books, a division of
Penguin Random House LLC, New York.

Doubleday and the colophon are registered trademarks of
Penguin Random House LLC.

Visit us on the Web! rhcbooks.com

Educators and librarians, for a variety of teaching tools, visit us at
RHTeachersLibrarians.com

Library of Congress Cataloging-in-Publication Data
Name: Atkinson, Cale, author, illustrator.
Title: Unicorns 101 / by Cale Atkinson.
Other titles: Unicorns one-oh-one
Description: First edition. | New York : Doubleday, [2019] | Summary:
Invites the reader to join top unicorn scientists as they clear up the myths and
misconceptions people have about these majestic creatures and their abilities.
Identifiers: LCCN 2018022372 | ISBN 978-1-9848-3036-4 (hc) |
ISBN 978-1-9848-3037-1 (glb) | ISBN 978-1-9848-3038-8 (ebk)
Subjects: | CYAC: Unicorns—Fiction. | Humorous stories.
Classification: LCC PZ7.A86372 Uni 2019 | DDC [E]—dc23

MANUFACTURED IN CHINA
10 9 8 7 6 5 4 3 2 1
First Edition

UNICORNS

You've seen them. You love them.
But how much do you *really* know about them?

Meet the top unicorn scientists working today!

PROFESSOR GLITTER PANTS

Grand Unistorian

PROFESSOR SPRINKLE STEED

Doctor of Magic

PROFESSOR STAR HOOF

Rainbowmetrics Specialist

PROFESSOR SUGAR BEARD

Certified Hornologist

Pete →

These unicorn masterminds—with the help of their trusty lab assistant, Pete—are here to bring the facts, settle the mysteries, and show us what the deal is with unicorns.

SECTION 1
What Is a Unicorn?

It takes more than a fancy horn to be a unicorn! Using Pete as our example, let's have a closer look at what a unicorn is like.

Common name: Unicorn

Scientific name: *Betterthan horsicus*

Family: MagicaHornidae

Size: Hoof to head, 30–67 hamsters tall

Horn: 4–20 rainbow meters long

Weight: 40,000 gummy bears

Colors: All of them

Group of unicorns: Cornucopia

Name for young: Candycorns

Life span: Super long

Did you know?

You can tell the age of a unicorn by counting the rings on the horn.

SECTION 2
Biology

A unicorn's key features are what separate it from the common horse, typical donkey, or unremarkable pony.

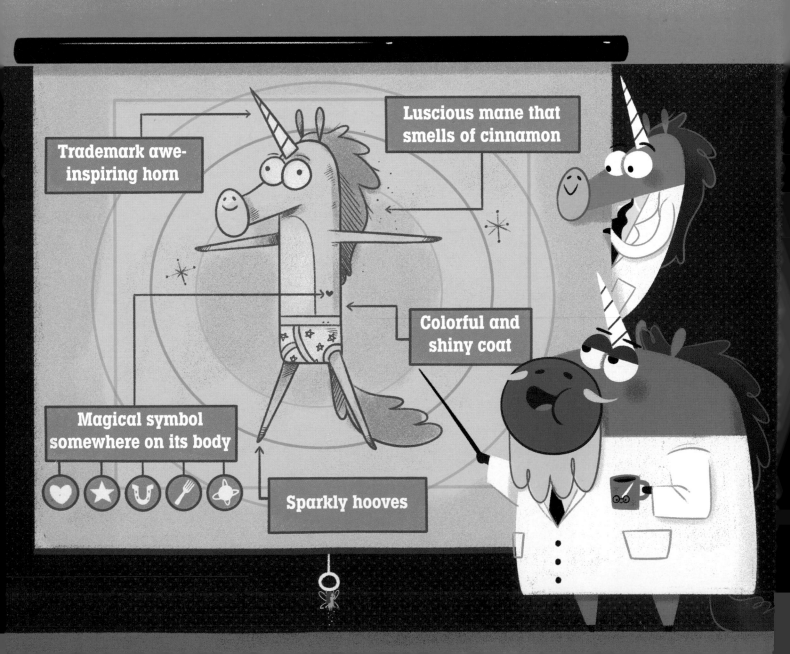

Trademark awe-inspiring horn

Luscious mane that smells of cinnamon

Colorful and shiny coat

Magical symbol somewhere on its body

Sparkly hooves

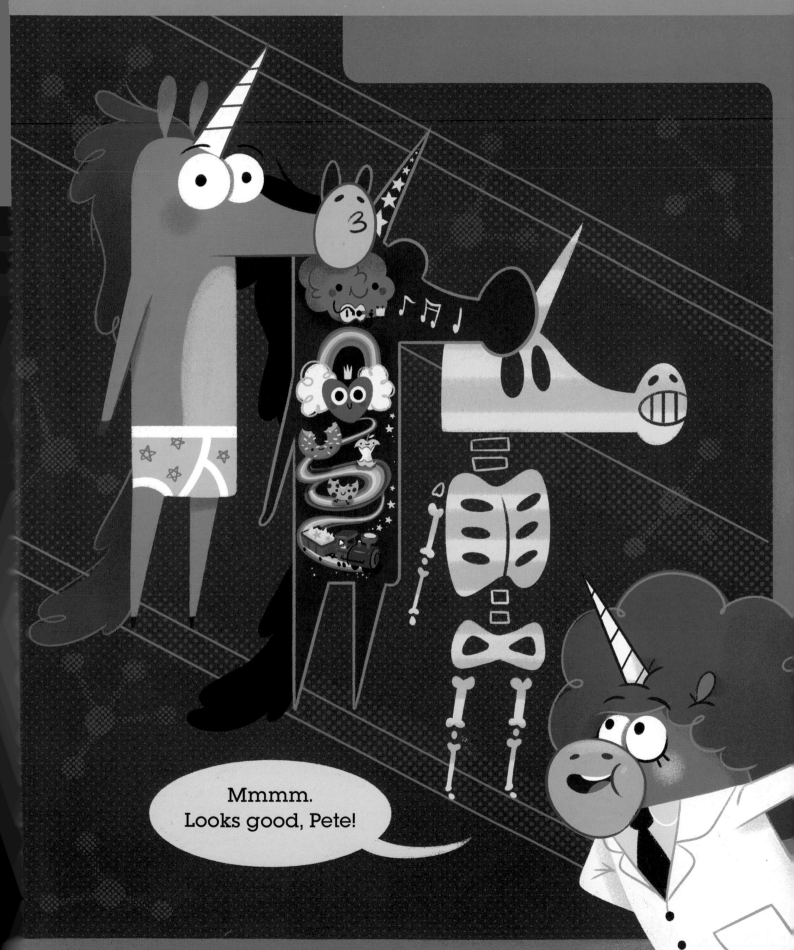

The Horn of the Corn

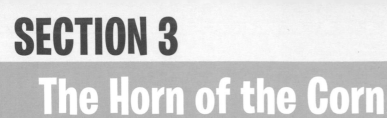

Unicorns are known for their legendary horns. Made of 50% magic, 45% mystery, and 5% sugar, unicorn horns are full of unknown and unpredictable powers.

Cases of unicorns accidentally using their horn's power include:

Sparks Sprinkletoot, 1990: Made it rain waffles for a full week.

Peppy Powerhoof, 1982: Made rainbows shoot out of the eyes of a chicken named Gus.

* Doughnut holder
* Tent pole
* Marshmallow stick
* Piñata smasher

SECTION 4
Diet & Digestion

A unicorn's diet is important to keep coats glittery, manes full, and horns strong.

While horses may be happy eating boring old hay, unicorns crave the finer things.

Things unicorns eat:

Ruby-and-emerald flapjacks

24-carat cake

Peanut butter and pixie dust sandwiches

Things unicorns avoid:

Salad bars

Cheese platters

Utensils

In the name of science, we need to cover what happens after a unicorn eats.

Professor Star Hoof, are you sure?!

I'm afraid we must. For science.

Like all other animals, unicorns have to go to the bathroom . . . with one slight difference.

Unicorns poop cupcakes.
Yes. Cupcakes.

This is why you'll never find a unicorn at a bake sale.

SECTION 5
Unicorn Types

Did you know there are a large variety of unicorns?

They include:

Siberian fur-corn

Miniature-corn

Muscle-corn

Super-horn-corn

Pug-corn

Mustache-corn

As we research and travel, new types are still being discovered.

Rare and exotic unicorns include:

* Zebra-corn
* Koala-corn
* Flamingo-corn
* Mer-corn
* Hamster-corn

SECTION 6
Unicorn History

Let's gallop back in time for a brief moment and learn where unicorns came from.

You can see here how, over the past million years, unicorns went from water to land and, eventually, to Pete.

Amoeba-corn

Fish-corn

Amphibian-corn

Lizard-corn

Dino-corn

Ape-corn

Horse-corn

Magesti-corn

Pete

Bird-corn

Fly-corn

Behold! Our gallery of history's most famous unicorns:

DR. HOOF SWEETMANE:
First unicorn to stand
on two legs

**PROFESSOR
SPARKS MOONDUST:**
First unicorn to harness
the power of the rainbow

JOLLY FANCYHOOVES:
First unicorn to wear clothes

BUTTERCUP SPARKLECHEEKS:
First unicorn to trot on Pluto

CAPTAIN CANDYBEARD:
Discoverer of the mer-corn

MONSIEUR BONBON:
First unicorn to
speak French

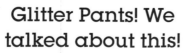

Glitter Pants! We
talked about this!

Habitat & Homes

Where does a unicorn live? Let's take a look at Pete's home to find out!

Three telltale signs you found a unicorn home:

1. Guard'n gnomes
2. Fairy infestation
3. Horn shape in doorway

HANG IN THERE, BABY!

HANG IN THERE, BABY!

SECTION 8
Social Behaviors

Social animals by nature, unicorns always enjoy chitchatting about the weather and discussing whose mane is brightest.

Favorite unicorn activities include:

Horn jousting

Competitive ringtoss

Javelin throwing

Knitting circles

But unicorns have a much more civilized way of solving disagreements:

the ancient ritual of **the dance-off!**

SECTION 9

Common Unicorn Questions

Why don't I ever see a unicorn?

Unicorns have become masters of disguise, in order to live a normal life and avoid being mobbed by "cornies" everywhere they go.

See if you can spot Pete hiding in these examples.

What does a baby unicorn look like?

There's a reason why you don't see baby unicorns. They are too cute. Well, not just "too cute." They are cuteness overload. Many people have been forever changed by the high level of cuteness!

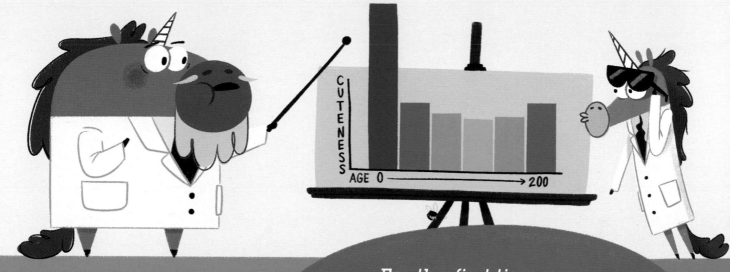

For the first time ever, we will give you a glimpse of a baby unicorn. *But be warned.* Stare too long, and you'll be seeing nothing but glitter for the next week. Prepare your peepers, 'cause here we go. . . .

Is it true that unicorns are the most magical creatures in existence?

> Yes. Obviously. As well as the most majestic, magnificent, and cool. Other notable magical creatures include pixies, corgis, and wizard yaks.

What do unicorns use rainbows for?

> The REAL question is, what DON'T unicorns use rainbows for? They paint their homes with rainbows, fuel their cars with rainbows, and even flavor their pancakes with rainbows! If you see a rainbow, you can bet your horn there's a unicorn nearby!

SECTION 10
Graduation Celebration!

CONGRATULATIONS! By completing this book and learning all the juicy unicorn knowledge, you have earned your white lab coat and now join the ranks of brilliant unicorn scientists! Welcome to the team!

Maybe you'll be the one to discover the next rare unicorn!